Confetti
the Magic Wedding Pony

For Oly, Ruth & Lucy, with love on your special day xxx – SK
For Florence, love Tatine – ST

SIMON AND SCHUSTER
First published in Great Britain in 2013 by Simon and Schuster UK Ltd
1st Floor, 222 Gray's Inn Road, London WC1X 8HB
A CBS Company

A CIP catalogue record for this book is available from the British Library upon request
PB ISBN: 978-0-85707-442-3
eBook ISBN: 978-0-85707-894-0
Printed in China
1 3 5 7 9 10 8 6 4 2

Princess Evie's Ponies

Confetti the Magic Wedding Pony

Sarah KilBride

Illustrated by Sophie Tilley

SIMON AND SCHUSTER

London New York Sydney Toronto New Delhi

At Starlight Stables, Princess Evie's ponies were enjoying their breakfast.

"What a perfect day for an adventure," said Evie.
You see, Princess Evie's ponies weren't any old ponies.
They were magic ponies! Whenever Evie rode them
through the tunnel of trees, she was whisked away
on a magical adventure in a faraway land.

A pretty white pony, with a long silver mane, nuzzled up to Evie.

"Confetti," said Evie. "Of course, you can come!"

Evie skipped over to the hay barn to get her rucksack
of useful things and find her kitten, Sparkles.
She could never go on an adventure without him!

They raced out of Starlight Stables
towards the tunnel of trees.
Where would it take them today?

They trotted into a castle courtyard, hung with garlands of roses. Princess Evie was now wearing a long silk dress edged with forget-me-not flowers. Confetti's mane was plaited with flowing ribbons and tinkling bells.

Waiting next to a carriage stood Princess Bella with her pet dragon, Loki.

"You're just in time," smiled Bella. "We're going to be my sister's

bridesmaids!"

How exciting! Princess Evie had never been a bridesmaid.

Just then, the castle doors opened and there was Bella's sister, Serena.

"How beautiful," gasped Evie.

Serena's long, white dress was covered with tiny diamonds and moonstones. She was wearing a glittering tiara with a delicate veil.

"You're going to be my special ring bearer, Loki," said Serena.

She tied a velvet bag to his collar with the two golden rings inside. Now they were ready to go.

Confetti's coat shone in the sunshine as she waited to take them
to the ceremony.

"You are the most beautiful wedding pony ever!" whispered Serena.

They were about to climb into the carriage when Bella looked worried.

"Where's Loki?" she said.

"We can't go without him," said Serena. "He's got the wedding rings!"

"Don't worry," said Evie. "We'll find him."

The bridesmaids raced back into the castle.

They searched for Loki in all his favourite places –
the cobwebby cellar, the warm greenhouse,
even under Bella's bed, but he was nowhere to be found.

At that moment, Bella and Evie
heard a tiny tinkling sound.

They looked up and saw Loki
on the chandelier, playing with
the glittering wedding rings.
"Loki!" called Bella.
But Loki wouldn't move!

"Wait," said Princess Evie, opening her rucksack of useful things. As she looked, some sweets fell out. Sparkles batted them from paw to paw.

"Do dragons like sweets?" asked Evie, hopefully.

"No," laughed Bella. "But they do love anything that's shiny."
As soon as Loki spotted the sweet wrappers, he dropped the
rings and swooped down from the chandelier.

"Quick, Evie!" said Bella, as she caught the golden rings.
"We haven't got a second to lose!"

They ran back to the courtyard with the wedding rings.
"Oh, thank you," said Serena, hugging them both. "Now we must get
to my wedding as quickly as possible. Everyone is waiting for us!"

Confetti galloped as fast as she could all the way to the wedding.

Serena's dress was so long and delicate, that Evie and Bella had to carry its train all the way down the aisle, towards the smiling groom.

The waiting guests all gasped when they saw the beautiful bride and her bridesmaids. The bride and groom put on the glittering wedding rings and made their promises to each other.

Bella and Evie threw rose petals up into the air and the happy couple smiled and kissed.

After the ceremony, everybody tucked into the delicious wedding feast. The guests enjoyed plates of honey pancakes, forest fruit fancies and Evie's favourite - apple blossom ice-cream! As the sun began to set, they toasted the newlyweds with blackberry bubbly.

"Now it's time for the fireworks," smiled Bella. Loki
flew up into the sky, leaving a trail of sparkling hearts.

Everyone cheered as the little dragon filled the sky with dazzling colours.

"These are the most magical fireworks I've ever seen!" gasped Evie.

When the fireworks had finished, it was time to go home. "Thank you for helping us," said Bella. The little dragon hopped up into Evie's arms and gave her a warm kiss.

"It was a pleasure," smiled Evie.
"Your fireworks were beautiful, Loki."

Princess Evie waved to Bella
and Loki, as Confetti galloped
through the castle grounds,
towards the tunnel of trees.

"What an exciting day," said Evie, as she took Confetti back to her stable. There, in the manger, Evie noticed a small parcel tied with ribbon and a silver bell. It was a piece of wedding cake, decorated with a spray of hearts.

"I'll always remember this adventure, Confetti!" said Evie.

"And how you helped to make it such a special day.

What a very magic wedding pony you are."

"Miaow!" agreed Sparkles.

Also available:

Shimmer
the Magic
Ice Pony

Neptune
the Magic
Sea Pony

Silver
the Magic
Snow Pony

Star
the Magic
Sand Pony

Willow
the Magic
Forest Pony

Indigo
the Magic
Rainbow Pony

Diamond
the Magic
Unicorn